WINNIE-THE-POOH
Gets Shipwrecked

BY VINCE JEFFERDS

A GOLDEN BOOK · NEW YORK

Western Publishing Company, Inc., Racine, Wisconsin 53404

Pooh was often heard to say,
"The lake is my favorite place to play."
Skimming pebbles was one of his tricks.
Another one was floating sticks.

But on this day,
It was sad but true,
He couldn't think
Of a thing to do.
(I suppose that
Sometimes happens to you.)

It was the same old lake, and yet
Something made him feel upset.
He was puzzled, for he could see
A place where the sky fell in the sea.

And that is what led Pooh to say,
"I'll make this a kind of exploring day."

So Pooh caught a piece of floating tree
And splashily set out to sea.
And as he paddled his log along
He sang his favorite exploring song.

"Exploring is fun for everyone
If you're doing something you've never done.
But exploring can be a dreadful bore
If you end up somewhere you've been before!"

Suddenly, the log split in two,
It was so old and rotten.
Thought Pooh as he fell into the lake,
"I don't want to explore the bottom!"

Pooh climbed out on a sandy beach.
His little raft floated out of reach.
"When they call it driftwood, they mean to say,
When you're not looking, it drifts away,"
thought Pooh.

Pooh sat thinking on the shore.
He remembered a story he'd heard before.
A tale of a sailor lost at sea.
"Why, that's just what has happened to me!"

The name of the story was *ROBINSON CRUSOE*.
If you haven't read it, I suggest you do so.

For dinner he could catch some fish,
But there was a problem with this wish.
If the fish should prove the winner,
Pooh might end up as the dinner.

Robinson Crusoe found fresh eggs,
So Pooh thought he might, too.
He spotted three beneath his legs
And thought, "What shall I do?
I must confess I never yet
Have learned to make an omelette.
Shall I have them boiled or fried,
Both of which I've never tried?"
Then the eggs made a cracking sound
And three little ducks rolled onto the ground.

The little ducks looked around at each other
And decided Pooh must be their mother.
"Shoo!" he said, "I'm already in trouble.
Mothering you will make it double."

But the ducklings peeped and raced around
Till Pooh fell dizzily to the ground.
And what d'you think that Pooh then found?

Pooh found a shovel, to his delight.
Indeed, it was a welcome sight!
For a shipwrecked sailor, an important thing
Is to dig until you find a spring.

Water! Water he must find!
Pooh dug and dug with that in mind.
But all he found was a mean old crab
Who gave his bottom a nasty grab!

Then he noticed something he hadn't before.
It appeared to be someone's front door.

Looking about, Pooh found a rock
And gave the door a gentle knock.
He woke up a clam. That's why
It squirted Pooh right in the eye.

Whereupon the clam clammed up
And then the wooden door slammed shut.

Pooh suddenly looked at the door. Then he said,
"Attached to that goat, it will make a great sled.
And then," he continued, "at least for a while,
I can travel around the island in style."

"Watch out for his horns! Slip it over his head!
Now this old door makes a very nice sled!"
The hole in the door was a perfect fit,
But the goat didn't like it, not one little bit.

As through the air our good friend flew
He was given a chance to learn something new.
The *back* end of a goat is dangerous, too!

Pooh started to walk and he tried to plan
The things he should do as a shipwrecked man.
But he couldn't think of a thing. Instead,
The thoughts tumbled wildly through his head.

At this point Pooh was startled to see
A set of footprints by the sea.
"Good! I'm glad I'm not alone.
Perhaps someone will take me home.
With luck," he said, "this may be my day.
These prints might belong to my man Friday."

Then he saw a second set.
He thought, "How silly can this get?
It's only one friend that I seek—
Can there be two Fridays in one week?"

The more he walked, the more prints he made.
And the sight of them made him more afraid.
He thought it would be most unpleasant
If he found there were monsters present.

"If there are monsters all about,
I'll need a fort to keep them out."

He gathered up
what junk he could
And built a little
hut of wood.

Inside it was dark,
except that a funny
Strip of light made
a line on his tummy.

Pooh was glad he had someplace to hide.
Then he heard a *Peep! Peep! Peep!* outside.
"Oh, bother," thought Pooh, "what a horrible din!
I suppose I shall have to let them in."

All of a sudden,
  to Pooh's surprise,
The floor of the hut
  began to rise.
A badger's head came up
  through the floor
And knocked poor Pooh
  out his front door.

The badger shouted, "Upon my soul!
You had the nerve to cover my hole!
Go somewhere else and make a start!"
And the badger kicked Pooh's house apart.

Now the sky grew dark and a wind came up,
And leaves and branches flew.
Pooh's tummy felt like an empty cup,
And I'll bet that yours would, too.

Pooh quickly dug a hole in the sand.
He didn't dig it deep.
He told the ducks, "It can't hold you.
There's just room for me to sleep."

Pooh slept little that scary night—
The howling made him weep.
But by the early morning light,
He finally fell asleep.

"It isn't like Pooh to stay out all night,"
Said Christopher to his friend.
"We'd better find him this very day,
Or we may not see him again."

Just then Eeyore
made an awful row.
He slipped and clanked
and stumbled.
"What have I put
my foot in now?"
The little donkey
grumbled.

Then they looked, and what he'd got
Was his right hind leg in Pooh's old pot.

The three of them looked everywhere
One could possibly look for a missing bear.
"Then," said Tigger, "if you ask me,
I'd say our friend has gone to sea."
So, traveling in naval style,
They rowed out to the distant isle.

They searched the island
    from end to end,
But saw no sign
    of their little friend.

"Peep!" went the ducks
As they hopped on the door.
"They are trying to speak,"
Observed Eeyore.

PEEP! PEEP! PEEP! PEEP! PEEP!

Slowly the door began to rise.
A startled Tigger jumped back in surprise.
"I'm sure it's a monster we're going to see!
Oh, why does this always happen to me?"
said Eeyore.

It was no monster, only Pooh.
"Oh, funny bear, we're glad it's you!
We worried about you all night through,"
    said Christopher Robin.

They piled in the boat, and the little ducks
Started making sad little clucks.
"This tiny boat won't hold anymore.
We'll surely sink!" exclaimed Eeyore.

Pooh said, "I think
    it most unkind
To leave my friends
    the ducks behind.
Where in heavens
    would I be
If they had not led
    you to me?"

"Don't worry," said Christopher, "ducks can float."
And he scattered some crumbs behind the boat.
Then they all sang the exploring song,
And the three little ducks all peeped along.